The Mystery of the Square Footprints

of the Square

by Kal Gezi and Ann Bradford
illustrated by Mina Gow McLean

 CHILDRENS PRESS, CHICAGO

Distributed by Childrens Press, 1224 West Van Buren Street,
Chicago, Illinois 60607.

Library of Congress Cataloging in Publication Data

Gezi, Kalil I.
  The mystery of the square footprints.

  (The Maple Street five)
  SUMMARY: While walking along the beach, five
children find a set of strange, square footprints that
lead them to a robot.
  [1. Mystery and detective stories]   I. Bradford,
Ann, joint author.   II. McLean, Mina Gow.
III. Title.
PZ7.G33902Mzb   [E]   80-10437
ISBN 0-89565-144-0

On sunny, summer days,

Linda, Vern, Tom,
Maria, and Barry...

liked to go to the beach. There, they could play in the sand. They could splash in the water. They could climb the rocky hillside with its many caves.

One late afternoon, the children decided to go exploring. Leaving the part of the beach where they usually played, they started walking along the shore.

After a while, they came to a lonely part of the beach.

"Let's turn back," said Maria. "It's getting late."

"Look!" Vern yelled and pointed. "Look there!" Vern was pointing to a trail of strange, square-shaped footprints.

"Wow!" screamed Maria.

"What kind of a creature would make such footprints?" asked Tom.

"I don't know, but they go up the hill," said Barry.

"Let's follow them and find out," said Linda.

Eagerly, the children followed the square footprints, footprints no human could have made.

Soon the hill became steep. Still, the children followed. They struggled from one big rock to another.

After what seemed a long time, the footprints led to a strange cave. Wild shrubs grew between the rocks and its opening. It was almost hidden from view.

"Ooh, it's dark in here!" said Tom, as the children followed the footprints into the cave.

"And scary!"

Suddenly, the children heard a ticking, like a clock! They heard the sound of a motor. The sound came from behind two tall rocks.

Fearfully, the children went toward the rocks, with Vern in the lead. "Be careful now," he said. Then, "Why . . . look at this! It's stuck! Between the rocks!"

The children saw a strange creature that was about two feet tall. Its eyes glowed. It hummed and ticked. Its feet were large and square.

"It's a robot!" said Linda.

"Right," said Barry. "At least, it looks like one!"

9

Now the children all talked at once.

"Where did it come from?"

"Could it be from outer space?"

"Could it be a spy robot? From another country?"

"Be careful! It could be dangerous!"

The children became silent then, watching the robot. It hummed and ticked on, but it didn't move.

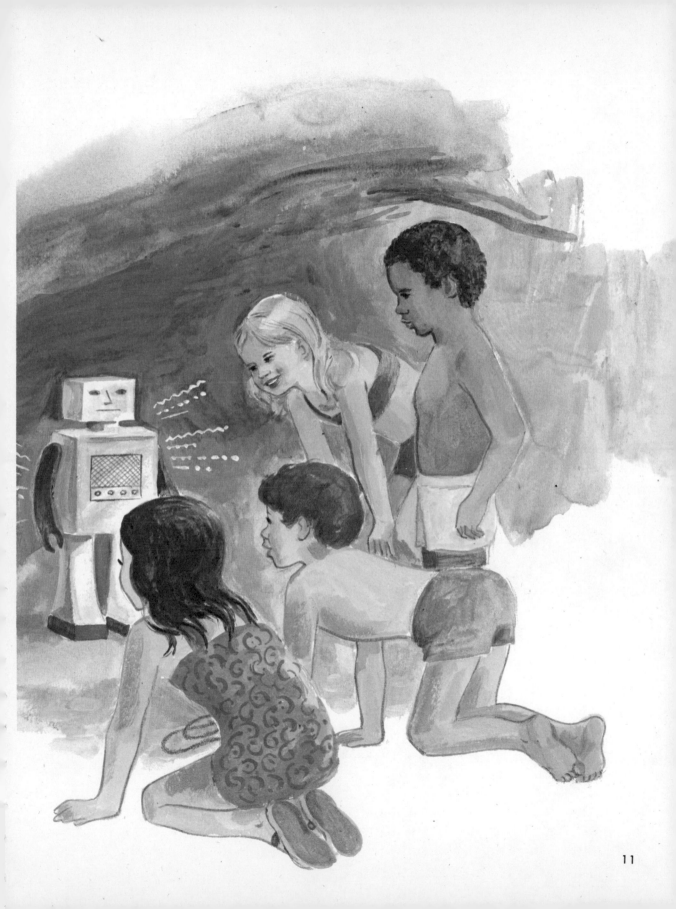

"What should we do?" Maria wondered. "It really is late! My mom will worry if I'm not home soon."

"Let's tie up the robot so it can't get away," said Barry. "I saw an old fishing net out on the hill. Someone must have thrown it away."

"And I have my rope," said Maria.

Vern and Barry ran outside to get the net. Soon they were back. They threw the net over the robot.

Maria unlooped her rope. She and Linda tied up the robot. Then they tied the other end of the rope to a rock.

The robot hummed and ticked. But it didn't move.

"Do you think that'll hold?" asked Vern. "My mother works in the science lab. I'll see if she can come back with us tonight. Maybe she can tell us what kind of robot this is."

As soon as Vern got home, he told his parents about the strange robot.

"You've been watching too much T.V.!" Vern's father said.

"You do have a good imagination," said Vern's mother.

"I didn't make it up!" said Vern. "Just come and see! I'll show you the robot!"

Finally, Vern's parents agreed to go to the cave.

15

After supper, Vern rounded up his friends.
Vern's parents and all the children got into the
station wagon. Soon they were at the beach.

They hurried to the lonely part, with Linda
in the lead. She was the first to enter the cave.

"Oh, no!" she shouted. "The robot is gone!" The other children and Vern's parents hurried into the cave.

"Are you sure there was a robot?" Vern's dad asked.

"Yes! Yes!" the children said. "Please help us find it!"

Vern's parents took out their flashlights. They looked around. "Look!" said Vern's mother. "Here are human footprints! And square footprints! Both are going away from the cave."

The group followed the footprints out of the cave and down the hill. Maria looked back. She could hardly see the cave now, in the late glow of the sunset's rays. On and on, the group went. The footsteps led to an old, beat-up cabin.

"Children, wait here!" Vern's parents said. Then the parents crept toward the cabin. From a side window, they looked in.

"Oh, my!" the children heard them say. The children were so eager to see what was inside! They moved quietly toward the window.

"Wow!" Barry whispered as all of them peeked through the window. The room inside was lit only by a portable lantern. Three teenagers were there. They had a remote control box. They were using it to give the robot commands. The boys made the robot stand, sit, stop, and walk in all directions.

"Amazing!" Vern's father said softly.

"That robot could be dangerous!" Vern's mother whispered. "We should get it into the lab to test it."

All of a sudden, the robot went crazy!
First it moved forward.

Then it jerked backward!

Then it went in all directions!

The teenagers struggled to control the robot, but it became worse. The robot pushed open the door of the cabin and started out. Then it made a fast move backward into the cabin. Finally, it ran toward a large bush.

The teenagers ran after it. The children and Vern's parents ran after the teenagers.

From behind the bush, several dark figures caught the robot. The teenagers stopped, fearful. They dropped their remote control box on the ground. And they ran away as fast as they could.

Now the dark figures moved from behind the bush. One of them was holding the robot. The group walked toward Vern's parents and the children.

"Oh!" Vern's mother suddenly cried out. "Dr. Bradshaw! Oh, my! Am I glad to see you!"

"Relax, men," said Dr. Bradshaw. Then, "Mrs. Preston! What are you doing here?"

Vern's mother told Dr. Bradshaw the children's story. At the end, he chuckled. "So my robot is your mystery, is it? It's something of a mystery to me too. You see, it's very new."

The children gathered around to look at the robot.

"I've been testing this robot," Dr. Bradshaw said. "I've been keeping it farther down the beach. I had a course for it to follow today. But it never showed up at the end.

"Those teenagers must have learned where I kept my robot. They must have made their own remote control box. It's pretty good for a homemade control. It changed the robot's direction!"

"How did you find the robot?" asked Vern. "When it didn't get to the right place, I mean."

"We traced its footprints to the cave, just as you did. Finally, we traced it here, to the cabin. We saw you outside."

"Why did the robot act so weird?" asked Maria.

"It got too many orders all at once," said Dr. Bradshaw. "Those boys were telling it to do things. I started telling it to do other things!"

Everyone laughed.

Then Dr. Bradshaw said, "How would you children like a tour of our lab?"

"Yeh!" the children shouted.

The next day, the children went to the lab. Dr. Bradshaw gave each one a small robot pin. Then the children went to the cafeteria. They had a great lunch. It was served by the robot himself!